The Pride Street Crew

9

Who Do You Love?

Mike Wilson

Published in association with
The Basic Skills Agency

Acknowledgements
Cover: Jim Eldridge
Illustrations: Jim Eldridge

Orders; please contact Bookpoint Ltd, 39 Milton Park, Abingdon, Oxon OX14
4TD. Telephone: (44) 01235 400414, Fax: (44) 01235 400454. Lines are open
from 9.00–6.00, Monday to Saturday, with a 24 hour message answering service.
Email address: orders@bookpoint.co.uk

British Library Cataloguing in Publication Data
A catalogue record for this title is available from the British Library

ISBN 0 340 77631 5

First published 2000
Impression number 10 9 8 7 6 5 4 3 2 1
Year   2005 2004 2003 2002 2001 2000

Typeset by GreenGate Publishing Services, Tonbridge, Kent.
Printed in Great Britain for Hodder and Stoughton Educational, a division of
Hodder Headline Plc, 338 Euston Road, London NW1 3BH, by Atheneum
Press, Gateshead, Tyne & Wear

JOHN / BONE

WESLEY / TALL

LUKE / SKY

SIMON / CUSTARD

CARL / SPOT.

I'm walking to school,
when Lisa Hardy runs up.

'Hey, Luke Sky,' she says.
'I like your new hair.'

'Thanks.'

'You look cute!'

I'm not sure if I want to look cute.
So I say nothing.

Lisa Hardy goes on:

'You know in books,
and on TV, Luke?
You know how they always say:
My friend wants to go out with you?
And you know how it always sounds so –
mega-gross?'
Then she says,
'Well – my friend wants to go out with you,
Luke Sky!'

I'm still saying nothing.

'Do you want to know who it is, Luke Sky?'
she asks.

I say:
'I know who it is.'

'Do you want to go out with her, Luke Sky?
Do you think she's a *babe*, Luke Sky?'

'Just stop it, Lisa,' I say.
'I'm not going out with Tamsin.
I'm going out with Lizzy.
Or did you forget?'

Lisa Hardy says:
'But you want to, Luke Sky.'

'And stop calling me that!' I say.

Lisa just smiles and says:
'You know you want to!'

Next Saturday,
I'm at work in the market.

Guess who comes to see me
on the market stall.
I'm lifting a sack of spuds onto the stall.
Just then I hear:
'Ooh! So strong!'

'Strong as well as cute, Luke Sky!'

I turn round
and there's Tamsin Taylor and Lisa.
Watching me.
Giggling.

They hang around all day.
Looking and smiling
and talking low to each other.

Uncle Ray thinks it's very funny
but I don't.

When it's nearly home time,
I slip out the back
to the rubbish bins.
I don't come back.

That night,
the phone goes at home.
'Young lady for you, Luke' says Dad.
'Another one …'

I take the phone.
'Where did you run off to, Luke Sky?'

Oh no.
'Tamsin …' I say.

'I just got a mobile phone, Luke!' she goes on.
'It's neat! My dad's paying for it!
And guess what – you're the first person
I called!'

'What do you want?' I ask her.

'Listen, Luke,' she says.
'Have you done your essay for Specky?
I'm stuck on mine. I need help.
'Why don't you come round
and help me with my biology?'

'I ... er ... I'm no good at biology,' I say.

'Well you can learn, Luke ...
I can teach you ...'

I hear Tamsin and Lisa start to giggle
as I hang up.

Two days later,
she phones me again.
I was just going round to see Lizzy
and I was late.

'Hi, Luke! It's me.
What are you up to?'

'Nothing.'

'Yeah,' goes Tamsin,
'I'm doing nothing as well.
Why not come out
and chill with me?
We can watch the cars go by.
Have you got any money, Luke?'

'No,' I say. 'Not till next Saturday.'

'So – are you coming, then?' she asks.

'No,' I say. 'I can't.'

'Don't you like me, Luke?' she asks.

'Don't know.'

'Do you hate me?'

'No.'

'Well, that's something,' she says.
'See you at school in the morning.'

'Yeah. See you Tamsin.'

So, I am 15 minutes late,
and Lizzy is not happy.

'Mum's out line-dancing,' she says,
'but she'll be back by 11.
What kept you?'

I say, 'Nothing.'

Lizzy and I were going to watch a video
but we can't agree what to watch.

She wants to watch *Romeo and Juliet*.
I want to watch *Alien Death Thing*.

In the end,
we just sit there all evening,
side by side.
Not saying anything.
Not watching TV or anything.

Just holding hands.

I go home
a long time before
Mrs Lawson comes back
from her line-dancing.

Next day at school,
Tamsin comes and finds me at dinner-time.
'What's up with you and Lizzy?'

'Nothing.'

'Come on, Luke,' she goes.
'You can tell me.'

'It's nothing to do with you,' I say.

'All good things must come to an end,'
says Tamsin.

I don't say anything.
So she says:

'You've got such sweet eyes, Luke Sky.'

Tamsin's mobile phone goes.
She opens it and listens.

'Not now,' she says.
'I'm with someone …'

She smiles.

'… I'm with Luke Walker,
if you must know …
Bye now.'

She puts the phone away.

'I hope that won't get you into trouble, Luke,'
she says.

'Who was it?' I ask.

Tamsin won't say.
She just smiles,
looks in my eyes,
takes my hand in hers.

She writes her name
and her new phone number
in the palm of my hand.
The dot over the 'i' in Tamsin
is a big heart shape.

She closes my fingers over,
and goes on holding my hand.

'If you need me,' she says.

If you have enjoyed reading about the Pride Street Crew, you may be interested in other books in the series.

It's Not The Winning
Carrot Rap
You Can't Be A Kid For Ever
She Likes Me
No Turning Back
Child's Play
Damp Dog
Let's Go Shopping
Make A Splash!
A Thousand Reasons
You're Never Alone With A Phone
Say It To My Face
Now I Know How It Feels